Sheep on a Ship

Nancy Shaw

Sheep on a Ship

Illustrated by Margot Apple

Houghton Mifflin Company

Boston

Library of Congress Cataloging-in-Publication Data

Shaw, Nancy (Nancy E.)
  Sheep on a ship / Nancy Shaw; illustrated by Margot Apple.
  p.   cm.
  Summary: Sheep on a deep-sea voyage run into trouble when it
storms and are glad to come paddling into port.
  RNF ISBN 0-395-48160-0   PA ISBN 0-395-64376-7
  [1. Ships—Fiction.   2. Sheep—Fiction.   3. Stories in rhyme.]
I. Apple, Margot, ill.   II. Title.
PZ8.3.S5334S1   1988   88-38183   CIP   AC
[E]—dc19

Printed in China

SCP   40 39 38 37
4500739623

To the friends and family members
who offered helpful suggestions

— N.S.

For Elaine, and Raymond and Kalle,
the sailors.

— M.A.

Sheep sail
a ship
on a
deep-sea
trip.

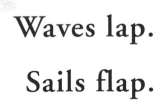

Waves lap.

Sails flap.

Sheep read a map

but begin to nap.

Dark clouds form
a sudden storm.

It rains
and hails
and shakes
the sails.

Sheep wake up
and grab the rails.

Waves wash across the ship.

Waves slosh. Sheep slip.

Decks tip.

Sheep slide.

Sheep trip.

Sheep collide.

Winds whip.

Sails rip.

Sheep can't sail

their sagging ship.

They chop a mast to make a raft.

Sheep jump off
their sailing craft.

The storm lifts. The raft drifts.

Land ho!

Not far to go.

Sheep come
paddling
into port.

Sheep jump off. Sheep fall short.

Sheep climb out. Sheep drip.

Sheep are glad to end their trip.